HOW THE WORLD GOT ITS COLOR

HOW THE WORLD GOT ITS COLOR

Adapted and Illustrated by **MARILYN HIRSH**

Crown Publishers, Inc. | New York

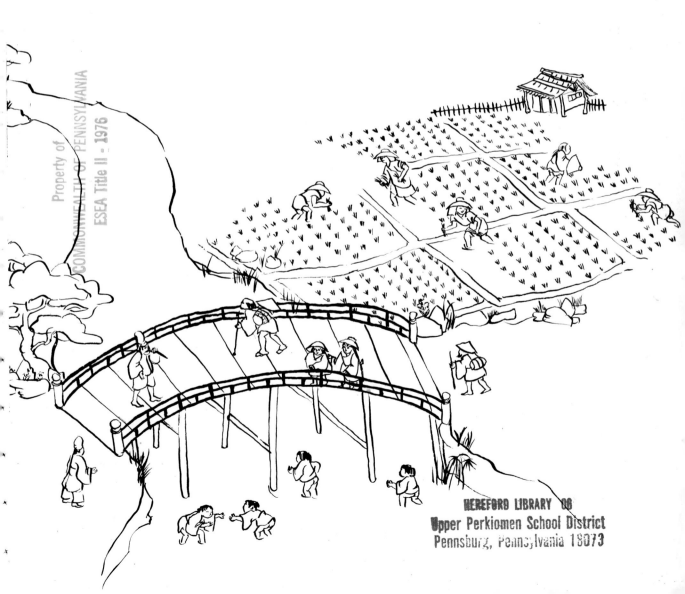

ALSO BY MARILYN HIRSH

Leela and the Watermelon
The Elephants and the Mice
The Pink Suit
Where Is Yonkela?

The text of this book is set in 16 point Aster. The illustrations are 4/color pre-
separated india ink drawings with overlays, reproduced in line and halftone.

For Sylvia, Justine and Joachim

There was a time when the world was half finished.
There were no colors anywhere except for

a set of paints which the
gods had given to an artist.

The artist painted every day
while his daughter Miki watched him.
As he used more and more color,
each painting became more beautiful
than the one before.

One day Miki's father went to offer his best painting to the gods.
He left Miki at home with her grandmother.

Her grandmother fell asleep, and Miki went to the room
where her father kept his paints.

The colors were more beautiful than anything she had ever seen.
She stared at them for a long time.

Then she slowly carried the paints outside.

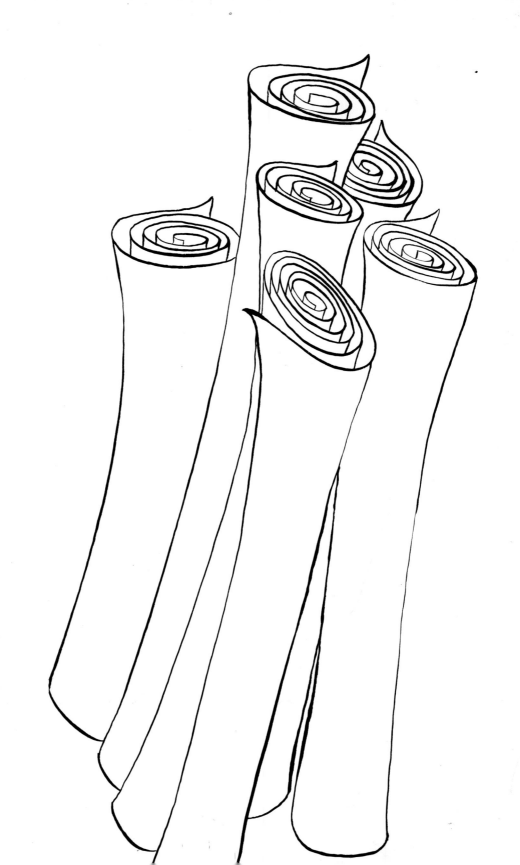

She took a brush and painted the poppies red, the trees green.

The rooster wanted his head to be red, and Miki painted the rest.

When Miki's father came riding home,
she was too busy painting her dress to notice him.

When he came near and saw what his daughter had done,
he roared with anger. All the earth shook.

The gods in charge of making the world
looked down when they heard the artist roar.

Miki was afraid,
but when she looked up,
the gods were smiling.

And as they smiled, Miki could see
colors appearing all around her.
Soon the whole world was colored,
and it has been that way ever since.